Folger McKinsey Elementary PTA
Adopt-A-Book

This book Adopted by:

The Stafford Family

Date: _December 6_ , 1996

David Delamare

CINDERELLA

GREEN TIGER PRESS

Published by Simon & Schuster

New York · London · Toronto · Sydney · Tokyo · Singapore

Ayoung merchant in search of his fortune moved with his wife and baby daughter to a fantastic city where watery streets wound this way and that, and people traveled in boats called gondolas.

The man spent all his savings on a small ship and a cargo of goods, and away he sailed to foreign lands to trade for silks, porcelain, and spices. When he returned to the city, he sold them all and bought another ship with the profit. So one ship became two, two became four, and four became eight. Soon the merchant had a great fleet sailing to ports all over the world.

He bought the grandest mansion on the grandest canal. There his wife and daughter, Ella, had everything they could possibly want, except the merchant himself. He came home only once a year, when autumn winds and tides brought his ship back from the Far East.

Ella grew into a bright, beautiful girl, soon to celebrate her sixteenth birthday. Her father sent presents—from Madagascar, a talking parrot; from India, a gold-and-emerald ring; from China, a carved mahogany puzzle box. But all Ella really wanted was for her father to come home for her party.

On her birthday Ella hurried to the balcony, searching the horizon for her father's ship. Not even the tip of a mast! Her hopes faded, but she was too sensible to let her birthday be spoiled.

Her mother hurried Ella into the garden. She had hired a traveling circus with acrobats, clowns, a magician, a fire-eater, and even jugglers, who filled the air with a shower of gold and silver stars.

Monkeys swung from bush to bush by their tails, chattering noisily. A burly bear pounded a drum, dancing clumsily to the music. There was even a baby elephant to ride!

Toward the end of the afternoon, as the sky turned a dusky purple, Ella saw a gondola drift slowly by. A boy her own age leaned on its railing, longingly watching the party.

Then the gondola turned and set a course for the palace across the wide canal. The boy looked at Ella and opened his mouth as if to call out, then smiled a wistful smile instead.

That night Ella sat in her window seat gazing at the palace across the canal. Her mother was reading to her as she had done every day since Ella was a baby. But Ella could not pay attention. She was thinking of the boy.

"Mother," she said, "did you see that boy in the gondola today?"

"That boy," said her mother, putting down her book, "is young Duke Fidelio, son of the grand duke. One day he may be grand duke himself."

"He seemed lonely," answered Ella. "I wonder if his father is as busy as mine." A tear rolled down her cheek.

Her mother came quickly to the window seat and put her arms around Ella. They sat quietly together, comforting each other, until it was long past both their bedtimes.

Ella's father came for his usual short visit that autumn, and then winter's cold gripped the countryside. A terrible sickness spread across the land. Ella's mother became ill and grew weaker every day. Now it was Ella who read to her mother from their favorite books late into the feverish nights.

Ella sent messages to her father by every departing ship. He came at last, bringing a famous doctor with him. But it was too late. Her mother slipped away that very night.

After her mother was laid to rest, Ella curled up on her window seat, thinking of happier times.

Suddenly there was a knock on the door. Ella's father came into the room and put his hand on her shoulder.

"Daughter," he said, "the winds are good and I must sail in the morning. There is nobody to take care of you now that your mother is gone, so I am sending you to a boarding school, where you will have other young girls for company."

Ella looked at her father with tears in her eyes.

"I wish there were some other way," said her father, "but it's a fine school, and I know you will be well cared for there." He kissed her cheek and then left the room.

Ella turned back to the window, staring through her tears at the palace across the canal. Now she might never see young Duke Fidelio again.

In the morning, Ella's things were put aboard a gondola, and she was taken away to school.

Two years passed. Then one day Ella got a letter from her father. He had married again, a widow with two grown daughters who would be like sisters for Ella. He wrote that her new stepfamily wanted her to leave school and come home right away.

As the gondola approached her house, Ella's heart beat anxiously. Would she like her stepmother and stepsisters? Would they like her? Then Ella caught her first glimpse of the home where she had spent so many happy years. Her spirits lifted.

Her stepmother and stepsisters were waiting on the landing. They wore identical frowns. Their lips puckered as if they had been sucking vinegar pickles. One look at those sour faces and Ella's spirits sank again.

Ella stepped out of the gondola and began to introduce herself.

"We know who you are," interrupted her stepmother. "Why else would we be waiting out here in the damp air? Now come along. There's no time for dillydallying. Take your baggage inside. There's work to be done!"

Ella soon discovered that she had been brought home to be their maid. From early morning, when she made breakfast and ironed their clothes, until late at night, when she washed their laundry and hung it to dry, she did nothing but wait on her stepmother and stepsisters.

The home she had once loved now seemed like a prison. Livia and Zenobia, her stepsisters, had moved into Ella's room. Ella slept by the kitchen hearth.

One morning Ella was sweeping the ashes from the fireplace. "Look," Livia teased, "she's all covered with cinders. She's a cinder girl—a Cinder-Ella!"

"Cinder-Ella! Cinder-Ella!" her stepsisters chanted. And that became her name.

Late at night, when she finished her chores and lay down wearily for a few hours of restless sleep, Cinderella wept for her mother and for the life she had once known in this house. She wondered if she would ever be happy again.

One day a messenger delivered a scroll with the grand duke's seal. With trembling fingers, Cinderella's stepmother broke the seal and unrolled the scroll. She shrieked and then called her daughters, who fluttered around her as she read aloud.

There was to be a masked ball! At the palace! The party was to celebrate the twenty-first birthday of Duke Fidelio, and all the merchant's household was invited!

"All the handsome young men will be there!" shrilled Livia.

"All the *rich* young men!" trilled Zenobia.

"Stepmother," said Cinderella timidly, "the invitation says all the household. Does that mean I may go, too?"

"Rude girl!" snapped her stepmother. "What do you mean by interrupting?" Then she laughed. "Of course you may go," she replied, "if you have all your chores done in time."

"Done in time, done in time!" taunted her stepsisters.

For the next two weeks the house was in an uproar. Gondolas came from shops all over the city, bringing silks, velvets, and brocades for dresses, masks, wigs, perfumes, pots of face creams and powders, and pair after pair of shoes and gloves.

Dressmakers worked frantically, cutting and sewing, nipping and tucking, trying to please the stepsisters, who were sure they could look slender and graceful—with just the right gown! The makeup artists had an equally impossible challenge—the stepsisters' permanently unpleasant pickle faces.

At last the day of the ball arrived. Carrying buckets of steaming water to wash the stepsisters' room, Cinderella met her stepmother, already dressed for the ball.

"Tsk, tsk," said her stepmother. "It looks as if you will never be finished in time."

"I only have this one last chore, Stepmother," replied Cinderella.

"Only one?" said her stepmother in her sickeningly sweet voice. "But I've just remembered. When you finish your sisters' room, you must clean the downstairs in case we bring guests home from the ball." She laughed and swept around the corner into the drawing room.

Cinderella sighed. She must have been dreaming to think she could go to the ball. What would she have worn? Her only clothes were ragged hand-me-downs from Livia and Zenobia.

Down the hall she could see her stepsisters making their final preparations. Livia clung to a dressing table as Zenobia pulled on her corset strings, tyring to squeeze in her sister's waist one extra inch. Livia gasped, ready to faint.

"What are you gaping at, Cinderella?" yelled Zenobia. "Run and get the smelling salts for your sister!"

Finally, Cinderella's powdered, perfumed, and overdressed stepmother and stepsisters stuffed themselves into the family gondola and set out for the palace.

Cinderella wandered sadly through the suddenly silent house and out on to a balcony. Across the canal lights bobbed on the water as gondolas arrived at the palace. The faint sounds of an orchestra floated on the night air. The ball had begun. Cinderella put her head down on the railing and wept quietly.

"Don't cry, daughter," said a gentle voice.

Startled, Cinderella looked up. A tiny, winged woman hovered in front of the balcony. Her gold hair shimmered with moonglow; her gossamer gown glittered with star dust.

"Who are you?" whispered Cinderella.

"I am your fairy-mother," she answered. "Your tears brought me here. And I know just what to do for them. How would you like to go to the ball?"

"The ball?" gasped Cinderella. "Oh, I have wanted that more than anything. But I can't go! What would I wear? How would I get there?"

"Leave that to me," replied her fairy-mother. "Now hurry to the garden and bring me the largest pumpkin in the patch."

How peculiar! thought Cinderella, but she quickly did as she was told.

The fairy-mother clapped her hands over the pumpkin. Swelling like a balloon, it floated over the balcony railing and dropped into the canal with a splash.

A fish leapt out of the water. The fairy-mother clapped her hands again. The fish fell back—growing, growing into a splendid fish-shaped gondola with the pumpkin for a cabin on its back.

A large rat, startled by the noise, scurried along the bank. Once more the fairy-mother clapped her hands. The rat sprang into the air and landed in the gondola—now a gondolier in a velvet-and-lace waistcoat. He was elegant, indeed, despite his long tail.

"Finally," said the fairy-mother, clapping her tiny hands in front of Cinderella, "a dress fit for a duchess."

Cinderella looked down and gasped. Her rags had become a glittering beaded gown. On her feet a pair of tiny glass slippers sparkled in the moonlight.

"Hurry now!" cried the fairy-mother. "You are already late! But you must return before midnight! At the last stroke of twelve, all will be as it was before."

The gondolier poled quickly across the canal and helped Cinderella out onto the landing. "Remember, miss," he said in a strange, squeaky voice, "I will wait until twelve—and not a minute longer."

A crowd of late arrivals swept Cinderella into the palace. She caught her breath. What spectacular costumes, what beautiful music! Suddenly, she noticed a tall man in a black cape and mask. He smiled and hurried toward her. "Excuse me," he said, "have I not seen you somewhere before?"

She was about to answer when a page came to the stranger's side. "Your highness," he said, "the grand duke asks that you lead the waltz." Why, it's the young duke! thought Cinderella, hardly daring to believe it was true.

"Would you do me the honor?" Fidelio asked holding out his hand to her. The orchestra struck up a waltz. They whirled about the ballroom, smiling, gazing into each other's eyes.

In a corner of the ballroom, Cinderella's stepsisters buzzed like angry bees.

"Who is that girl?" pouted Zenobia. "She's keeping the young duke all to herself. I want a turn."

"*You* want a turn?" hissed Livia. "He wouldn't look twice at you! It if weren't for her, he'd be dancing with *me*!"

"Smile, girls," snapped their mother, "or *no one* will be dancing with either of you."

After a time Cinderella and Fidelio strolled out into a quiet garden and stopped by the side of a reflecting pool. Cinderella stared into its mirror-smooth waters. Could the beautiful woman looking back at her really be poor, shabby Cinderella?

Fidelio began to talk about what it was like to grow up as the son of the grand duke, about how lonely court life had been for him as a young boy, and about his years of study at the university. And then he told her how he longed to find someone to share his life.

"Now I want to know everything about you," he begged. Cinderella's heart sank. How could she tell him of her horrid life with her stepmother and stepsisters?

She turned away, ashamed. Then, out of the corner of her eye, she caught a glimpse of the palace clock tower. The clock was about to strike midnight!

"Forgive me," she cried, "but I must go at once!" She rushed toward the garden entrance.

"Wait, please wait," Fidelio called after her. "I don't even know your name!"

Cinderella bolted down the stairs toward the landing. She stumbled, losing one of her glass slippers, but then regained her balance and ran on.

The gondolier helped her aboard, and then began poling rapidly across the canal. A sudden wind churned the water into rough waves. One . . . two . . . three . . . the clock was striking! Cinderella stared frantically through the darkness toward the other shore.

Four . . . five . . . six . . . Looking down, she saw that her beautiful gown was turning to rags.

Seven . . . eight . . . nine . . . "Please, can you go any faster?" she called. The gondolier turned his head as if to answer. Cinderella gasped. He was changing back into a rat! His beady eyes gleamed fiercely.

Ten . . . eleven . . . The gondola melted away under her feet, plunging her into the icy water. She swam for shore.

Twelve! Dazed, Cinderella sat on the bank. Gradually, the water quieted and the moon came out from behind a tattered cloud. A fish glinted in the moonlight and then splashed into the water. Pieces of pumpkin bobbed on the ripples.

Cinderella shook her head. What had happened? Had any of it been real? Then, to her astonishment, she saw still on her foot the other glass slipper.

As she settled near the fire in the kitchen to dry her clothes, Cinderella hugged the slipper tightly to her heart. She would always have it to remind her of this magical night.

The following afternoon, as Cinderella served tea in the parlor, her stepsisters could talk of nothing but the ball.

"It was boring and awful," complained Livia. "Why, no one asked us to dance the entire evening."

"And the young duke danced every dance with the ugliest, clumsiest girl I ever saw," sniffed Zenobia.

"And now he's all in a tizzy," said Livia, "because she ran off before the ball was over. He's ordered his pages to search the countryside. He says he'll marry the girl whose foot fits the glass slipper she left behind. What nonsense!"

Zenobia lifted her skirt to reveal a fat foot resembling a large potato. "Can't you imagine me a duchess?" she gloated.

"Certainly not!" snapped Livia. "However, I *can* imagine me as one." And she stared admiringly at her own fat foot resembling an even larger potato.

A knock at the door interrupted them. There stood a page from the palace, holding the glass slipper on a satin pillow.

"I am commanded to find the maiden whose foot will fit this glass slipper," he said.

"Let me try it, let me try it!" cried Zenobia, sticking out her leg.

"But, madam," said the page, staring at her potato foot and then at the tiny slipper.

"Fit the slipper!" demanded Zenobia.

The page sighed, knelt, and held out the slipper. Zenobia pushed her toes into it. She grunted and groaned and wiggled her foot, but it would go no farther.

"Perhaps, madam, the slipper is just a touch too small?" suggested the page.

"One last try," panted Zenobia. But try as she might, she could not get her foot all the way into the tiny glass slipper.

"Now me, now me!" shouted Livia, wagging her potato foot at the page.

"Oh, dear me!" said the page, shaking his head. He sighed again and held out the slipper.

Livia shoved her toes into it. She grunted and groaned and wiggled her foot, but it would go no farther.

"What about that other young lady?" asked the page, pointing at Cinderella.

"One last try," panted Livia, leaning back in her chair and pushing with all her might. Suddenly, with a sharp *crack,* the slipper shattered into a thousand pieces.

"Oh, my," cried the page, "the slipper! It's gone! Now Duke Fidelio will never find his true love. I'm afraid his heart may shatter just like the slipper!"

Cinderella smiled, took the other glass slipper from her apron pocket, sat down, and slid her foot easily into the slipper.

Her stepmother and stepsisters stared in horror while the page clapped his hands with delight. Then he ran to the garden and set a torch blazing that could be seen from the palace across the canal.

At once a gondola left the palace and headed across the canal to the garden landing. Fidelio leapt ashore.

"So it was you!" he exclaimed, taking Cinderella's hand. Then he laughed. "How many nights I have gazed across the canal at this house, dreaming of the girl I saw here long ago!"

Cinderella laughed, too. "And how many nights I have looked across the canal at your palace," she said, "dreaming of the boy who sailed past the garden on the day of my sixteenth birthday."

"We have so much to talk about . . ." began Fidelio, only to be interrupted by loud, angry voices as Cinderella's stepmother and stepsisters came galloping toward them across the garden.

"Please, Fidelio," cried Cinderella, "let's leave here at once!"

They hurried to the gondola and set out for the palace, where they were married the very next day.

Cinderella's stepmother and stepsisters never recovered from the shock. The more they thought about Cinderella's good fortune, the more jealous they became. They lived long and unpleasant lives, and never stopped complaining.

Fidelio and Cinderella, on the other hand, lived long and very pleasant lives. Their love blossomed and grew deeper as the years passed, and when they were older they became good and kind rulers. The city of watery streets prospered under their reign, and for all we know, that delightful city may be floating there still.

For M.O.

GREEN TIGER PRESS, Simon & Schuster, Rockefeller Center, 1230 Avenue
of the Americas, New York, New York 10020. Copyright © 1993 by David Delamare.
All rights reserved including the right of reproduction in whole or in part in any form.
GREEN TIGER PRESS is an imprint of Simon & Schuster. Designed by Alan Benjamin.
Manufactured in the United States of America. 10 9 8 7 6 5 4 3 2

Library of Congress Cataloging-in-Publication Data
Delamare, David. Cinderella / by David Delamare. p.   cm.
Summary: In her haste to flee the palace before her fairy-mother's magic
loses effect, Cinderella leaves behind a glass slipper. This version
of the traditional fairy tale is set in a city of canals and gondolas.
[1. Fairy tales. 2. Folklore.] I. Title. PZ8.D3695Ci 1993
398.2—dc20 [E] 92-25126 CIP ISBN 0-671-76944-8